Lisa Ferland

Yana Popova

WE WALK THROUGH THE FOREST

We WALK through the forest

TWEEDLE EE DEE.

Let's LOOK all around,
do you see what I see?

It's a cute little birdy
that's SINGING at me.

And its song is so sweet.

TWEET,
     TWEET,
          TWEET!

We SING through the forest

TWEEDLE EE DEE.

Let's LOOK all around,
do you see what I see?

It's a cute little rabbit

that's HOPPING to me!

And it's happy to jump.

THUMP,
THUMP,
THUMP!

We HOP through the forest

TWEEDLE EE DEE.

Let's LOOK all around,
do you see what I see?

It's a cute little
lizard that's
SLINKING by me

And it quietly slinks.

TINK,
　　TINK,
　　　　TINK...

We SLINK through the forest

TWEEDLE EE DEE.

Let's LOOK all around,
do you see what I see?

It's a cute little butterfly
FLITTERING free

We FLIT through the forest

TWEEDLE EE DEE.

Let's LOOK all around,
do you see what I see?

It's a huge grizzly bear
down beside that old
tree

And it quickly eats lunch!

MUNCH,
MUNCH,
MUNCH!

We SNEAK through a clearing.

The bear doesn't see.

Let's LOOK all around,
crouching down on one knee.

We run through the meadow,

we're nearly home free.

Then we hide on the hill.

STILL,

STILL,

STILL.

We HIDE on the hillside

TWEEDLE EE DEE

Let's LOOK all around,
do you see what I see?

It's our kind-hearted mama who's running to me

With a kiss and a hug. SNUG, SNUG, SNUG.

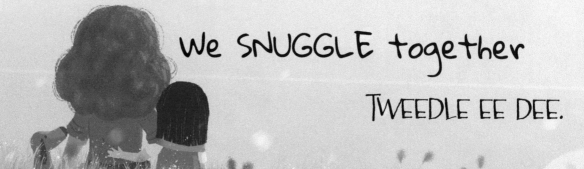

We SNUGGLE together
TWEEDLE EE DEE.

Let's LOOK all around,
do you see what I see?

Together   with   MOM,

we're

as SAFE
as can be.

"So, what gave you a scare?

SHARE,

SHARE,

SHARE!"

``WELL...

We SANG through the forest,   'TWEEDLE EE DEE.'

We HOPPED and we FLITTERED

around an old tree.

Then we SAW a big bear who was really furry.

So we HID on the hill,

STILL,

STILL,

STILL."

We STAND all together

TWEEDLE EE DEE.

Mama LOOKS out ahead,
"Do you see what I see?"

She squints her eyes tight and
points to a tree.

Emerging from the forest of spruce,

We see—

not a bear—

but a silly old MOOSE!

THE END

DEDICATED TO

C & L – MY ADVENTUROUS OUTDOOR EXPLORERS. – LF

ALL LITTLE ADVENTURERS. – YP

WE WALK THROUGH THE FOREST

CPSIA information can be obtained
at www.ICGtesting.com
Printed in the USA
LVHW070356180723

752486LV00008B/381